Lover Lines

Annette Pateman

Pateran Press

Pateran Press

UK
Canada

Lover Lines

ISBN 978-1-7773416-3-3

First Edition

Cover Design by picmatic0
Line Art by Lilyanti Suryaningsih

www.worditry.com
Find Annette Pateman on Facebook, Twitter, Instagram and
YouTube

Dear readers,

'Lover Lines' is my second collection of poetry.
In this book I look at love, relationships, and
some of the effects the Pandemic has had on relationships.

Annette Pateman

Acknowledgements

Thank you to my husband John who has given me the space to write
Thank you to my children
Lianne, Joe and Saskia

Table of Contents

love

Basket Weaver

My dreams are built upon a basket made of palm fronds
Beaten and wetted in the river until they become soft and
supple, like a woman waiting for her lover.

The basket motif coloured and dyed with dreams
of love and life
Created to draw the eye of the casual observer
the passing customer

Cheek

Do you remember the day when you first placed
Your cheek on mine?

That was the day I knew I had come home...

Doth thou love me true?

I put my hand
in thine,
and thought that
you were mine.
Doth thou love me
true?
If only I knew.

Dark Haired Maiden

A dark haired maiden
Whose tresses lie against her
Back like smooth dark silk
You carry a soft warm heart
The empathy and love you
give sets you far apart
From others who would
if they had the chance
tear you apart

Stand unbowed in the wind
and the storms that arise
without sight
Put thine hand in mine
and by my will it
will all come right

Fair haired Maiden

The memory of a fair head maiden
has oft wandered with me.
Tearing down the walls of my soul.
Etching away the peace of my mind
Oft doth the memory of you assail me.
Appearing like the morning dew,
on a rosebud in the faint spring sunshine.
Although I would that the memory of you
leave me.
I know I would lament the loss.
For thou art a part of me.

Happiness

Happiness is being with you
Going for a walk in the woods
Looking out and seeing the silver moon
High in the sky after a day spent with you
Happiness is looking forward to the sunrise
And another day to spend with you

I will see you again

I will see you again
I WILL see you again
I will SEE you again
I will see YOU again
I will see you AGAIN

Left

I am the one that
is left on the tree.
The one with the bruise on the skin
that they choose not to see.

I am the one that is
left on the tree.
Hands touch and stroke
and then pass by me.

I am the one that is
left on the tree.
Round and full
and ready to be plucked.

I am the one that falls
to the ground.
I roll and stumble
and bounce around.

I am the one
that sought out fertile soil.
Whose roots scrambled,
for dew drops and water.

I am the tree that
holds up the
fruit, that others
look at and pick over.

Lover Lines

The lover lines pour from his pen
He dips the nib into the ink,
begins again
A new sentence to tell of his love
His want of her
His need

The Lover Lines flow from his pen
Today is a good day
She returns home
He will see her
again

He closes his journal on the
Lover Lines therein
Opens the locket which contains
her picture

The Lover Lines
Settle into his heart
Where they will remain
Never to depart

Lovers Rock

This reggae music,
Smooth and sweet as rum and raisin fudge,

South London shabeen.
Empty room in an abandoned house with a basement.
All that is needed is a DJ, reggae records,
Curry goat and rice and peas and the sweet smell
Of herb.
Of course, the people

My back against the wall...paper
As my partner and I dance the 'rub.'
The wallpaper fades a little, as it rubs against my back.

This is the time of the
night moves.
Wicked tunes.
Choooon.

*Shabeen is the word commonly used to describe an all night
reggae dance.
The word is thought to have originated in Africa.

Loves You More

I am the one who loves you more,
who stands at the gate and
waits by the door.

I watch for your smile
the dimple arrives,
but none but me would keep the score.

There exists a 'she' between our past,
our future, present
perhaps till the last.

I wish that I could change
my fate,
from the one that came too late.

For she had already taken your heart,
and held on to it,
never to part.

So, I am the one who waits by the gate,
resigned and accepting,
I swallow my fate.

The Day after Valentines Day

Red and pink foil chocolate wrappers litter the
love seat where we sat and said I love you and
exchanged Valentine's Day cards and watched
a romcom on Netflix

The Great Lovers

There was
Romeo and Juliet
Cleopatra and Mark Antony
Lancelot and Guinevere
Tristan and Isolde
Paris and Helen
Orpheus and Eurydice
Napoleon and Josephine
Odysseus and Penelope
Then there was
You and Me

The Letter

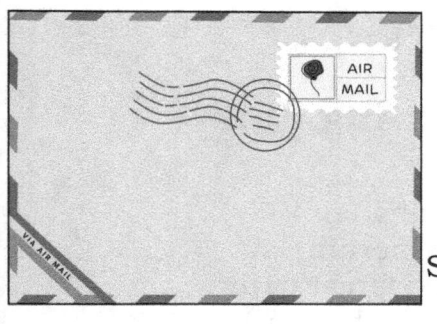

I waited by the banana tree,
where you first saw me.
I shaded sun under the leaves.

Watched as others got letters
from foreign.
Saw the faces crack brilliant smiles.

Hands grasping paper
that meant they were going.
Bodies gyrating with joy.

I waited by the banana tree
where you first saw me.
Wondering why your letter
did not find me.

Was the one you called more special than me
was she more cultured?
More beautiful?
Was her skin softer than mine?
Was she more woman than me?

The answers never came.
You never explained.

I waited by the banana tree,
where you first saw me.
As she sauntered pass me unknowing,
her body freely swaying.

Going to the market,
to buy things for foreign.

Twas Upon A Morning Fair

Twas upon a Morning fair
We decided to take the morning air
We meandered along the forest path
Sunlight filtering through the grove
With the bluebells growing by the great oak

Then you knelt beneath the bower
Of that steadfast old tree
Going down in bended knee
You took my hand in thine

These were the words you uttered to me

Will you marry me
Will you accompany me
Through this life of vicissitudes and change
For you are the person who moves me

I looked into your eyes and replied,

You are the one whom I will love
All the days and moons of my life
Though pattern shift and shadow lengthen
I will love you
Till I am no more

Wonder

Sometimes I wonder what would happen if I left you
Really left.
Packed my bags and took my certificates
I wouldn't leave those behind
I worked too hard to get those
What would happen if I just left
Walked away one day
The thought is my waking fantasy
I walk away from all of it
Away into a parallel dimension
Which for me is freedom on this earth
Maybe eventually living with another person
But we have so many memories together
So many years
Not all the time was bad
We laughed a lot together
I'm not sure what we laughed about, but laugh we did
We talked about the state of the world
We tried to solve some of those conditions
Over the kitchen table
In the kitchen
What to do
I know not

You Love Me

You love me
I know you do
You love me
I'm sure you do
You love me
You said you do
Yay!!!

Love Of The Environment

Lake Day

Today is a day for joy.
Water splashing.
The air is humming and the camera clicking.
Trying to capture the heart of the day.

A granddaughter floating in her pink blow up boat.
This is the first time.
A grandson with a fistful of sand
Testing the water.
A beautiful teenage granddaughter,
Swimming in bright red lipstick.
Hindu, gold, Shiva medallion,
around her neck.

Loon Song

The loon sits high in the tree
Singing
Lonely me
My mate
Come and find me

Loon sits high in the tree
Singing
Maybe it's my time
Mate come and find me

Loon sits high in the tree
There beside him
Sits his family
Singing

Loon Song
Loon song
Come hear my
Loon Song
Soon
I will be gone

Mango

He hands me a ripe mango
He smiles shyly as he offers it to me.
I take it and look at it.
I notice this mango has brown skin.
Darker than mine.
He is waiting.
Waiting for me to bite into this sweet gift.
I bite and gold yellow mango juice runs down my Chin.

Sublime on my tongue.

Thank you Devon
I say to my cousin, when I have wiped
my mouth with the back of my hand.

The Land

The land was old and wily.
Spirits roamed over the deeps of the face.
Some were benevolent.
A soothing patient touch.
Remembering kind hands and soft voices,
that kneaded the loams of their hearts.
Planted and pulled out weeds.

The angry spirits their maws open
in a not silent scream.
Gave clods of dry earth from which
nothing planted came.
Their dutty broke backs and shovels,
their soils dust became.

This land now willed to those who don't
understand it.
Who poke and prod and take from it,
while giving nothing back.

The angry spirit,
maw open.
Able to lay in wait for centuries
with basilisk stone eye
half closed.

If you take and take
then I will seal your fate,
and unto me like dust you shall return.
I will await my turn

*Dutty is an African word for earth

Family

Brother

How is it possible to know
a brother, who died before I was
even born.

And yet,
I do know you brother.
I hear your laugh.
A soft chuckle which
makes dimples and then
It's gone.

Your voice a quiet rain.
Your movements,
smooth and precise.
A quiet gentle person.
Thoughtful.

Isn't this why people
love you?

My uncle who is almost
the last of my mother's
generation,
talks about you still.

Even in this conversation on his
birthday,
he talks to me about you.

You are loved still,
brother.
I know you.
A person of balanced feature and form.
I know you even though you died before
I was even born.

You were a person who listened well,
and loved his mother.
A person who was dutiful.
That most old fashioned of words.
Which is big and loud in meaning
yet deep and quiet with action.

I also love you brother.
Even though you died before
I was born.

Written for my brother Glen.
Glendell Howell Lawrence

Brothers

I am so lucky to have you brothers
Tall, dark and handsome you ar
So many talents and gifts you have
The world may try to deride
We laughed and sang and played
Family games galore
We went to church regularly
then we went to church some more
One among you had the gift of technical drawing
A beautiful singing voice
The other could draw and sketch amazing portraits
And a giving heart rare to find and behold
I will always love you
My brothers
Black men now in the world
You will surely
Live the good life you deserve
I love you my brothers

Mother

My mother is soft and hard.
Her hands are Warm.
She is sweet like,
hard candy.
She is not
Pink.

Sisters

You remember don't you
Laughing while we painted
On the lipstick and swapped
Purses and clothes
Argued over who would
Wear the red nail polish
and who would wear the
Last brown panty hose
You remember covering for
Me with mother and I did
The same for you with father
Leaving school a lesson early
To meet the boyfriend on time
You remember eating candy
Celebrating Easter, Bonfire night
and Christmas
Visiting cousins in Kings Heath,
Birmingham
Visiting cousins in South London
Our mother's side the Lawrence
Our father's side the Moseley
The Blackwood and the Morris
They are also there too

Going to school hand in hand
Having hair plaited and parted
Bantu knots, cornrows, single plaits
and afro, up do and lions mane
All the hair styles to look good
In our search for the right boy,
the nice boy
The one that would be
Approved
All the while reggae music playing
Church hymns singing
Sabbath keeping in the pews
So many memories sisters
That bind us in family love
Even now that mother and father
Are gone and can no longer
Prove or disapprove
We live on and we remember
the things that we were taught
I love you my sisters

*Bonfire night, celebrated on the 5 th Nov remembers when
Guy Fawkes tried to set fire to the Houses of Parliament in
the UK. An effigy is made of Guy Fawkes and the effigy is
burned. Bonfires are lit and fireworks displays take place.

There Was A Child

There was a child.
She died coming forth,
Screams loud in her ears

Alive till the last.
The womb her tomb.
The channel the path
that led nowhere.

The womb truly an empty vessel.
Tick tock tick tock.
The body can bear no fruit.
Arms do not hold a child.

And yet a life of sorts.
Sun rise and sun set marking the days

Nothing can change
the inner malaise.

Sadness is a cold voice.
It asks for the days of my life
as it's price.
Yet I don't want to pay the ferryman.
The coins can't quite leave my hands.

Tomorrow is a new day
and it brings a small hope.
Everyday is different,
Yet everyday is the same.

Barren is my name
and my time is barren.
There remains time and I will wait.

Fear

Drove Past Me

Is it you that
drove past me and shouted
an obscenity?

Is it you?
Why not show your face?

Are you afraid to come near
for fear of your fear?

Is it you who drove past me
and shouted an obscenity?

Polygamist

I am the second wife.
I live in the house and scrub the floor.
But when the first wife is out,
you shut the door,
I am the second wife and more.

You fall on my breast
and tumble me on the floor.
I have no real station,
the first wife is at the door.

Call me by my first name,
slave no more.
I am the second wife,
when the wife goes out the door.

I cast my eyes downwards,
gentle hands when I am near her.
These feelings inside me
knock at me insistently

Tonight you will come to me,
and I will fall and acquiesce.
My heart will bloom inside me
And then shrivel like all the rest.

I am the second wife.
Unwilling heart of this poly life.
For you can never admit me to the light
and give me a true life.

Ring

Your ring.
A brand on my hand
strangling my heart.
A chokehold
That tears me apart.

Sweet looks and touches
hides and covers
the thoughts beneath.
The need to hurt me
like a crave to eat.

The sun shone brighter
in the sky below,
a beauteous blue.
You smiled, you coaxed,
you gentled me.

But then hard look
hard voice, hard mind.
It was as though I was blind.
Not seeing the real you.
The blade heart that
Would cut me in two.

Now I wish to run and hide.
To wonder why I am still alive.
To endure this endless pain.
What do you have to gain?

Tomorrow is the day I leave,
this relationship that makes me bleed.
But then you smile and it seems like love,
your grip on me a skin tight glove

The blow comes out of the blue.
What did I do to hurt you?.
You fell me like a fresh cut tree,
I am down and out at your mercy.

I gather thought from the mess.
Pack a bag and leave the rest.
Today is the day I go,
reclaim my life and strike a bow.

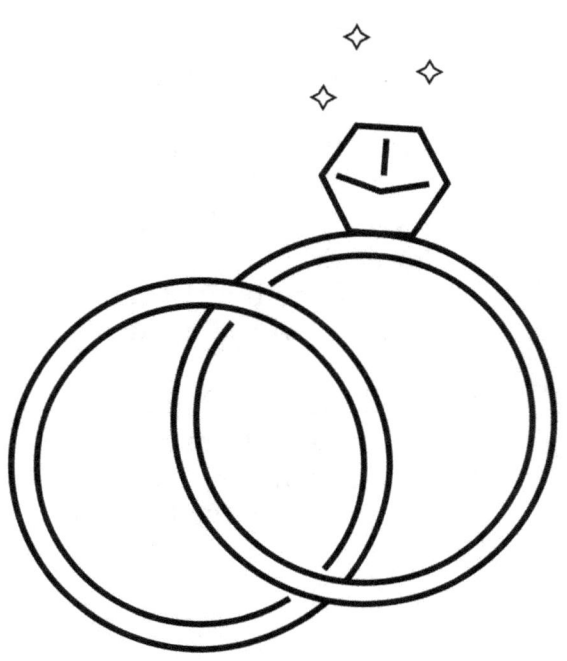

For Shame

For shame

My heart cried that you had
chosen her
Over me

For shame

Was she not a plain Jane,
and already in a relationship
with another

For shame

Would you unsettle
our planned
life
for this other

For shame

All the promises you made me
melt away like yellow butter
on a warm day

What to Do or Falling

What to do when the sea
rushes in, and the breakers
rush over the outcrops of
rock, sharp and pointed.

What to do when the edge
of the cliff looms too too near, and the
fall is close enough to touch.

What to do when the
tear falls down unbidden
and the heart flutters in the
chest unasked.

What to do when the breath fails
and rushes too fast through
and through.

What to do when the eyes
look and keep looking,
searching, blinking wide.
What to do when the
swallow constricts and wants to hide.

My my what a day,
what a night.
Secret looks, secret slights.
My my what slight
my my what a flight.

Fly fly away into the night.
Out into the sweet sweet air where
the roses bob and
the lupine fly,
out and away
a long oversight.

Wall 2100

I go to the wall
A high mesh fence
Electrified to keep animals out
Animals like me
It is dark but I think I can see a shape moving
I inch closer
Yes, it's her.
My daughter,
Her pale face looks pinched and worried
With good cause.
In this time 2100
A time of walls and barricades
Black is separated from white.
Surveillance through electronic eyes
that turn and watch for movement
Of animals like me is,
everywhere.
But even this hyper vigilant and punitive
state can't look everywhere at once.
So my daughter has found a space where once a month,
once in a full moon.
She can approach the fence that separates,
the black from the white

She nods her greeting
Wastes no time in passing me a parcel.
It contains
food supplements
Medicine
Things I can not access easily on my side.
Also a letter for me from her.

I give her a letter also.
We write in code.
We cannot risk detection.

At last after the exchange is made
and what seems like an age we can talk.
We have about ten mins.

The children are well.
Monsignor Peterus is in poor health
and so the white side
Is unsettled

This can be a dangerous time for everyone
Factions calling for change can gain ground.
Blood can be shed as people fight
for a foot hold.

I nod with understanding.
I point to the sky at the moon.
That at least has not changed.
It is our signal to leave.
I see her weak smile.

We make the sign that says.
I love you.
She pulls up her hood and
moves quickly away from the wall.

Until the next time.......

Xenophobia

The xenophobe
A man or a woman
Gender of no concern
A person who wants to keep
the familiar
The sky
The ground
The houses and all around
Must be familiar
Essential to wellbeing
This belief that this is how the world
Should be found, this is the world at is best
The same unchanging
Predictable
False structure for safety
Same people
Same thought
Same dress
Same void
So when the new enters
It is cast out
As other
As spore
As contagion
As threat
As swarm

As foreign
As invader
As looter and plunderer
As criminal
As taker
Until there is nowhere to rest
The head of new
They must cast out
Or be destroyed
Bit by bit
Little by little
Drip drip
Tick tock
Until they are worn away
Worn down
A shadow
A spectre
Seemingly there
Not really aware of how to live
Anymore
Xenophobia
A disease
That feeds on fear and
Creates otherness

You Don't See Me

You look at me
Yet you don't see me
You touch me
But you don't feel me
You hear me
But you don't listen me

Flash Fiction

A Good Day

That day we walked hand in hand together in the park
Then we went to the supermarket.
When we got home we were
Tired and so we decided to order a take out meal.
That day with you was a good day

Almost

I stand by the water and look out across the lake. I know you
are here. Always with me.
I reach out a hand my fingers outstretched and seeking. I
can almost feel your kiss.
Right there. On my cheek.

Coffee Shop Love

The coffee shop was crowded that afternoon when you
decided to tell me.
You said,

'I thought the feelings would go away'
I listened unknowing.
You continued,

'I married her because we had grown up knowing each other.
We went to the same school. Our parents worked in the
same factory and were close friends. I knew that I was
attracted to men, but I tried to ignore it. So we got married
and had three children. I think she knew all those years.
Fifteen years.'
You then said,

'I met Harry at work. It was a very slow courtship, if you
want to call it that. In the end I couldn't deny it anymore. It
was three years before I admitted to myself and to Harry that
I had feelings for him. I decided I had to be honest with
Helen, and so I told her within weeks of admitting to myself
that this was how I felt. That I was a gay man. She was
devastated, but said she had known that something was
missing. She said she knew that something was not quite
right between us.' In the end Helen has accepted that we are
not right for each other. Of course she is still an important
person in my life. She is dating again and seems happy with
Rob, a man she met at work.'

This was how I learned that my best male friend was a gay
man and that he was in love with a man named Harry. I
looked at him and noticed as if for the first time, the smile he
had that lit him up from the inside. The happiness that
shone through his eyes and out into the world, for all to see.
I felt a contentment inside me, knowing that my friend had
found happiness and could live his truth.

Full Moon

You worked with me to put the kids to bed. Afterward we
stood beside the large picture
window and looked out at the full moon. You asked me if I
remembered the night you had said you loved me
I said yes, of course I remembered. I asked you if you still
loved me the same.
You said, yes you loved me the same as then, and even
more.

You asked me,
Do you still remember the night I said I love you
I said,
Yes, I remember of course
I asked you,
Do you still love me the same?,
You said,
I love you the same as then and even more

We two people, lucky to have found each other
Held hands and went
Up to bed...

Going To Dance

Getting away to go to shabeen wasn't easy.
Dawn had been extra good that day. Helping her mother in
the kitchen.
Going the extra mile. Her sister knew she was up to
something and gave her a knowing look before returning to
the book she was reading. Dawn had even tidied the
bedroom she and her sister shared. That was when her
sister knew she was planning something.

That night when everyone was asleep. Dawn shook her
sleeping sister gently awake, to tell her she was going out to
a dance. She said she was going to a shabeen, an all night
dance. Dawn said that her sister had to cover for her, incase
she wasn't back before mum came to call her downstairs for
church.
Sister listened carefully and watched bemused as her sister
picked out her large brown afro, donned her stiletto shoes
and pencil skirt. This was the fashion of the day that
doubled for church and for party wear, if it was teamed with
the right blouse and hairstyle.
She followed her sister quietly downstairs, and watched as
Dawn climbed nimbly out of the front room ground floor
window. Of course she would cover for her. Her sister had
taken extra precautions. Leaving one of her mother's
hairdressing heads in her bed with the covers drawn up.
Sister laughed quietly to herself, wondering what her parents
would say, if they knew that Dawn had gone to an all night
dance.

Dawn was planning to dance the night away with Royston,
whom she had met when she was out running a shopping
errand for mother. She had told her sister that she and
Royston were in love. Royston was always buying her gifts of
perfume and expensive creams. Dawn shared these gifts with
her sister, who at eighteen years of age was a bit older than
Dawn, but didn't have a boyfriend.

• shabeen is an all night dance

Hands

A glance across at the hands resting on the soft blue blanket
shows a scene of life. The skin spreads loosely over veins
that rise like twisted roots. Thoughts and memories move
and coalesce in the mind. Going back to a time when the
skin on hands and face was youthful,
fresh and smooth.
With the passage of time come the memories that bind
together. Joined in a union called marriage. Another glance
down shows hands resting gently on a soft pink
blanket. The fire in the wood burning stove flares briefly,
then returns to a steady orange and
yellow burn. Breath can be heard slowly moving between the
two people seated before a fire and sharing this scene in
their life.

Ice On His Back

Gerard had been alone for a long time. Today he felt that loneliness keenly.

Most days he was fine, but today he felt that his life had been reduced to a tall stack of failed relationships. One relationship atop the other.

First there was Marina. He had loved her so much, but they had both been so young. They hadn't really realized how special their relationship was until it was too late, and she had left for another city.

Then there was Efua. The thought of her beautiful dark skin and her laugh could still make Gerard smile with memory. Her parents hadn't really approved of the fact that he just wanted to date their daughter. They had wanted him to declare his 'intentions' and at that time, his only intention had been to have fun and to be around Efua.

The parental pressures and Efua's own insecurity had got the better of the relationship in the end. So they parted, and went their separate ways. The following year he heard on the grapevine that Efua was engaged to an accountant. Gerard knew that he could never have competed with that. He hadn't been ready to settle down then.

Then there was Amina. She had been petite, beautiful and passionate. She was also an illegal immigrant. She was also somewhat younger than Gerard, but they had got on so well. Although their backgrounds were very different, they had made each other laugh and provided a safe harbour for each other. In the end the past caught up with Amina. She decided to go back to her home country, rather than live with the threat of deportation. Gerard had been heartbroken, but by then the relationship had become very complicated. Amina had been having a long distance relationship with another man. It had felt as though their love had been under attack.

There were other relationships of course, but these were the ones that caused him to lose sleep sometimes. Of course there had been the short fleeting relationships. The ones that were great for a month, but then just fizzled out.

Now he was in the pandemic lockdown and Gerard felt the weight of those relationships. The memories of them pressed down on him. He felt himself shiver with thoughts of love and loss, the chill of them like cold ice on his back.

The Ship

The ship moved through the water.
Angela watched as the water parted as if in two sections,
before the great bow of the ship. Almost like she imagined
that the parting of the Red Sea would be like when Moses
stretched forth his hand. She felt happy. She felt secure.
Melvin had arranged her passage on board this ship. They
were sailing away from all that was familiar yet oppressive to
them. They no longer fit in that place they had once called
home. A place where they couldn't be together. Melvin was
from a higher class. He wasn't supposed to be with Angela
who was beautiful, kind and clever, but the daughter of a
man who did honest work with his hands.This wasn't the
way things were at this time. So they had talked and plotted
and planned, and then planned some more. Till Melvin had
said a sort of goodbye to his parents. Parents who had
rejected Angela when he had at last told them about her,
and his intention to marry her. Angela had found it easier to
leave. Her mother was sad to see her go but wanted the best
for her daughter snd saw that she was unhappy with things
as they stood.

So Angela and Melvin stood by the railing of this great ship.
Holding hands and happy, if a little apprehensive about the
future. They had made it. They were together. They had the
future to look forward to. All would be well. They would work
it out together.

Skinny Jeans

Michelle had packed her outfit into her school rucksack safely concealed underneath her books. There it was. The skinny jeans and the blouse with the t shirt that declared her to be 'Black and proud.' She wondered for a moment, what her parents would think if they knew that instead of going to her cello lesson, she was right at this moment donning lip gloss. She was meeting Derek after school. He didn't have to get changed. All he needed to do was remove his school tie. They were both in grade 13 having stayed on at school. Parents just didn't understand Michelle thought restlessly. Michelle knew she was in love. What she felt for Derek was real. There time together was precious because they had both applied to college, and who knew if they would both get into the same one. So Michelle went into the ladies washroom, in the cafe by her school, and squeezed into her skinny jeans. She put on the T-shirt with the confident slogan, checked her lipgloss, shrugged on her rucksack and walked quickly to the square, where Derek would be waiting.

The Proposal

The proposal came not with with him on bended knee.

Brian had brought a nice, moderately expensive meal at a restaurant that was good
but not overly special. He had made the effort to wear his best jacket and comb the errant lock of hair that fell across his forehead, frequently obscuring his light brown eyes. Glenys had made an effort of course. She always did. Her dark curly hair had been curled and pinned so that it formed a soft halo around her head. The effect was very fetching and Brian wondered how he had managed to catch the attention of this special woman.

The waiter approached the table and asked if he had enjoyed the meal and the wine. Brian wondered irritably why it was always the man they asked. He would have liked to know what Glenys would say, about the medium dry red they had ordered to go with the meal. They had both decided on the choice of wine. Brian liked that. He liked the discussion. He liked the sharing, and he wanted to share more experiences with Glenys. He was tiring of driving across the city to visit Glenys, at the house where she lived with her parents.

So he had decided to propose. He had proposed to two women before with no success.
This felt different. The relationship that had developed with Glenys felt richer and deeper somehow. So he cleared his throat and took a sip of water because he wanted a clear head and Glenys really was very distracting. Particularly when she smiled and lifted her eyes to look directly at him.

He started by asking what she thought of living with someone.

He watched carefully as she spooned the rum and raisin ice cream her favourite dessert, into her mouth. He felt a twinge of disappointment when she said she had lived with someone and was not disposed to doing so again. The experience had been heartbreaking for her and left her with a young son, and the decision to return home to have the financial and emotional support of her parents.

Brian then asked what she liked about him. He wanted to know what she valued in their relationship. He waited with expectant breath, as she said she felt quite deeply about him. She felt safe with him. She also mentioned that her son quite liked him, and that was important to her. He let out the breath he hadn't realized he was holding at that point. He smiled. Glenys smiled. He took hold of her hand and moved to kiss the soft brown knuckles, absently noting the red nail polish on her nails.

A warmth grew in him and he said,
" I have a house, a car and steady job. I can give you and your son on a good life. Will you marry me?"

He watched intently as Glenys paused. She smiled. She looked into his eyes and said.
"Yes I will marry you"

So it was that Brian and Glenys got engaged and later married a year and a day later, in the old English church that stood in the middle of Brian's village.

Trigger Warning

Today Fran watched a film series on a
popular streaming website.
She has a membership to the streaming service
and enjoy films.
Something they both enjoyed. Before.
Something that even now has the power to take Fran away.
So they watched a series together. Seated on the sofa..
The sun setting outside. Fran noticed the orange and pink
banded colours of the darkening sky, through the french
windows. Then the screen lights up and the film begins.
Fran is sucked in quickly. Carried away on the roller coaster
ride that is the film story. Suddenly there is the betrayal. A
woman is left heartbroken. She retaliates by
sleeping with another man. All is well for a time,
but eventually she and her husband
Have 'the talk'. This is where it all goes awry.
The ugly argument.
A man supplanted by another man. A woman betrayed.
Intense scenes.
Fran is triggered, triggered, triggered.
It hurts but She can't really feel it. She can't really feel it.
Fran starts to feel it.
In her chest. In her heart. In her head. A fizzing and fuzzy
clouded thinking.
Muddied colours. Yes. She can feel it Triggered and trigger-
ing. Enjoyment in the film
melted and gone. It is too close to her. No space between
Fran and it. No fresh air.
The air grown heavy suddenly. The room is too quiet. It will
be over soon.
The film. It will end soon. Fran means the film. Honestly.
She means the film.
Will end soon.

Pandemic Themes

Alone

The lockdown and the Pandemic
Left me alone
Adrift in a sea of closed doors
Walls all around
No friend knocks the door
No lover to be found
All masked up
Lips hidden
Muffled sound
Dreams of courtship
Have gone away
I hope to find my love
Another day

Dating App

The dating app blinked
And winked
Faces going past in a line
Like a conveyor belt
Will I find the love of my life?
If I look closely enough
Will my future partner signal
Their presence to me

Human Touch

Memory lanced
through him like
Ice on his back
He saw her face
Her smile
Even her hair with its
Intricate dark braids

He shivered with loneliness
It had been too long since he
Had experienced a hug
Felt human touch
Seen a true smile.

The dating apps left him
Empty and wanting
Full of promise
But actually a false hope
In this time of Pandemic

Meal

Sharing a meal with my love is special
More special now
Than before
Watching him chew and swallow
Enjoy the food which although not
As tasty as our favourite restaurant
The one we frequented in our 'before'
Pandemic life
Is still satisfying somehow
Perhaps even more than before

Menu

The menu of life is spread out
So much to choose from
The veritable smorgasbord is dizzying
The diamond that is the perfect match
Sparkles yet cannot be found
Hope shines eternal
The right partner to find
The Pandemic a roadblock
That is there to be climbed
Oh love where can you be?

Mysterious Breath

This is a serious time
People are losing their lives
In Pandemic woes
I cling to my lover and
He clings to me
We have each other
I'm grateful for that
Celebrate life
Mysterious breath
It is a gift
We know that

Not Alone

Lucky to have you here
I'm not alone
Not on my own
Fortunate to have you here
Company to me in this lockdown
A help meet
My mate
My love
I'm lucky to have you here
I'm not alone

Pandemic Retreat

Lockdown has put us into retreat
We have retreated from the world
You and I
Me and my Pearl
We sit entwined on the soft cushions
Of the living room love seat
We watch films on the internet
The cinema has closed it doors
Standing side by side in the kitchen
We rediscover the solace of
Home cooked meals
We find ourselves together in
This Pandemic Retreat

www.ingramcontent.com/pod-product-compliance
Lightning Source LLC
Chambersburg PA
CBHW072044170626
46811CB00008B/3149